Not too young
and other stories

Nelson

Thomas Nelson and Sons Ltd
Nelson House Mayfield Road
Walton-on-Thames Surrey
KT12 5PL UK

Nelson Blackie
Wester Cleddens Road
Bishopbriggs
Glasgow G64 2NZ UK

Thomas Nelson Australia
102 Dodds Street
South Melbourne
Victoria 3205 Australia

Nelson Canada
1120 Birchmount Road
Scarborough Ontario
M1K 5G4 Canada

© Thomas Nelson and Sons Ltd 1991
Editorial Consultant: Donna Bailey
'Not too young' was written by Griselda Gifford and illustrated by Pat Nessling
'Jan's birthday' was written by Jill Kent and illustrated by Anna Hancock
'Benjy's pictures' was written by Catherine Storr and illustrated by Gareth Floyd

First published by Macmillan Education Ltd 1987

This edition published by Thomas Nelson and Sons Ltd 1992

I(T)P Thomas Nelson is an International
        Thomson Publishing Company

I(T)P is used under licence

ISBN 0-17-422528-8
NPN 9 8 7 6

Printed in China

Not too young

Selina was tired of being too young.
She was the youngest in her family.
The others were called James, Jill,
John and Jenny.
Selina was tired of going to bed first.
    "I am tired of being too young,"
she said.
"I want to go to the shop on my own.
The others go there on their own."
    "You are too young," said her mother.

Selina ran into the garden to cry.

"What is the matter?" asked an old lady
who was looking over the fence.

"I am tired of being too young," said Selina.

"I was the eldest in my family,"
said the old lady.

"Sometimes I was tired of being the eldest,"
she said. "Come to tea with me and
I will tell you about my family."

So Selina asked her mother and
her mother said that she could go to tea
with Mrs Brown.
Mrs Brown gave Selina cake and
sandwiches and a big cup of tea.
"It is hard to be the youngest,"
said Mrs Brown. "But it is even harder
to be the eldest."

"I had to look after the young ones,"
she said.

"You went to bed later," said Selina.

Mrs Brown laughed.

"I was too tired to stay up long," she said.
"I had to help with the meal and wash up."

Selina thought about it.
Her brothers and sisters helped
more than she did.

"I miss my big family," said Mrs Brown.
Selina smiled at her.
"I shall come and see you often," she said.
So she went every day to see Mrs Brown.
They became great friends.
In the summer, they had tea in the garden.
When winter came, they sat in
Mrs Brown's warm kitchen.

But one cold winter's day, Mrs Brown
did not come to the door.
Selina called through the letter box.
Mrs Brown still did not come.
Selina found a box to stand on.
She looked through the kitchen window.
Mrs Brown was lying on the floor.
Selina wondered what to do.
She found a little window open and
she got through it.
She ran over to Mrs Brown.
The old lady did not move.

Selina put a blanket over Mrs Brown.
She must get help.
She looked at the telephone.
Dial 999 for an ambulance, it said.
Selina dialled the number.
"Mrs Brown is ill," she said.
"She is lying on the kitchen floor."
The ambulance soon came and
the men took Mrs Brown to hospital.
Selina watched the ambulance go and felt sad.

Next day, the doctor from the hospital
came to see Selina.

"You were just in time," he said.
"Mrs Brown was very ill. The blanket
kept her warm. You saved her life."

"Little Selina saved the old lady's life,"
said James and Jill and John and Jenny.

"She is not a baby any more,"
said their mother.

"Then can I go to the shop
on my own?" asked Selina.

"Yes," said her mother, laughing:

"Hurray!" said Selina.

When Mrs Brown came home
from hospital, Selina took her friend
some sweets from the shop.

"I can go to the shop on my own now,"
she said. "I am not too young any more!"

Jan's birthday

    Today was Jan's birthday but
Jan was still fast asleep in bed.
It was just light outside.
Mum and Dad were already up.
Dad was a window cleaner and
he had to go to work.
He drove a blue van with
a long ladder on the roof.
Dad waved goodbye to Mum and
drove off in his van.
He had a lot of windows to clean that day.

Mum went into Jan's room.

"Wake up!" she said. "Time to get up and get ready for school," she said.

Jan was still sleepy.

"Get up Jan," said Mum. "It's your birthday."
She gave Jan a big hug.
Jan jumped out of bed.

"It really is my birthday today,"
she said and gave a little jump for joy.

"Yes," said Mum. "Hurry up and
get dressed, then come down for
your birthday breakfast."

When Jan went downstairs, she found
her brother Martin had made the breakfast and
her sister Liz had laid the table.
By Jan's place there were lots of letters.
Jan opened them and stood all
her birthday cards up on the table
in front of her.
    "Thank you all," she said.
She felt very happy.

After breakfast, Liz had to leave for
her school and Martin had to go to his work.
Jan helped Mum clear away
the breakfast things and she put
her cards on the shelf.

"Hurry up Jan," called Mum, so
Jan took one last look at her cards and
then got ready to go to school.
Mum was ready to go to work too, so
they both left the house together.

When Jan got to school,
the bell was ringing.
Jan was just in time and rushed into
her class room.

"Happy birthday Jan," said her teacher.
Then the class sang "Happy birthday Jan.
Happy birthday to you," and they gave her
a big card with all their names on.
Jan was very happy.

Jan sat down at her desk.
After a while she felt sad and began to cry.

"What's the matter Jan?" said her teacher.

"Well, my Mum wished me a happy birthday
when she woke me up this morning, and
my sister Liz and brother Martin got me
a birthday breakfast and they wished me
a happy birthday. But my Dad
went to work before I got up.
He forgot all about my birthday!"

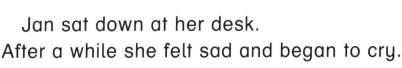

Just then there was a noise at the window.
Tap, tap, tap! Tap, tap, tap!
"Whatever can that be?" said the teacher
and they all looked at the dirty windows.
"There's someone outside!" said Jan.
"And he's writing on the window!"
said her teacher. "Look, it says
'Happy birthday Jan'," she said.

"Dad! It's Dad!" cried Jan.
"He's come to clean the school windows."

"And he's come to wish you happy birthday,"
said her teacher and she opened the window.
Jan's Dad leaned in.

"Happy birthday Jan," he said.
"You see I did not forget!
I went off to get your birthday cake.
You will find it in my van."

So Jan went out to the blue van and
in the back she found a big cake.
Dad gave her a big hug and
wished her happy birthday again for luck.

Then Dad finished the school windows and
Jan gave everyone a piece of cake.

"What a lovely surprise," she said.
And so it was.

Benjy's pictures

"We are all going to paint pictures today," said Miss Wills.

"I shall paint a man mending a car," said Tessa.

"I shall paint a tiger eating a fat lady," said Ruth.

"I shall paint a long, long train going into a tunnel," said Joe.

"I shall paint a big lion behind a tree," said Benjy.

All the children began to paint.
Tessa's car was very good.
It looked just like a real car.
Ruth painted a very fierce tiger.
Joe's train had a driver and
lots of big wheels.
   "All three pictures are very good,"
said Miss Wills.

But Benjy's picture was a mess.
The lion did not look like a lion and
the tree did not look like a tree.
Then he upset the water over the paper.
Benjy was sad and angry.

"Why can't I paint a real picture?"
Benjy said to his Mum that night.
"I can see things just as well as my friends."

"You see a lot," said his Mum.
"When we lost the grey kitten you found her behind the cupboard."

"And when I lost my tie pin, Benjy saw it on the carpet, looking like part of the pattern," said his Dad.

"Benjy sees too much," said his sister Rose. "He saw me take Mum's lipstick when I was dressing up."

"And I saw a furry caterpillar that was
climbing up Aunt Emma's back when
we had tea in the garden," said Benjy.
"I didn't tell Aunt Emma.
The caterpillar was orange and black
with tufts of yellow fur.
I liked that caterpillar a lot better than I
like Aunt Emma," said Benjy.

Sometimes Benjy saw things that
other people did not see.
There was a patch of dark colour on
the wall above his bed.
Rose said it was nothing at all.
But Benjy knew it was a crocodile with
a long tail and a mouth full of
sharp crocodile teeth.
It kept Benjy safe at night when
he was fast asleep.

There was a round wooden ball on
the bannisters at the foot of the stairs.
It had a little hole in one side.

"I think it's the eye of a pirate,"
said Benjy.

The pirate winked at Benjy when
he went upstairs, so Benjy drew
a long nose under the eye.
He drew a mouth under the nose to
make him look even more like a pirate.
But Mum was cross and washed it off.

One day Benjy's Mum was going to cook the dinner.

She tipped some oil into a pan.

Then she put the pan on the cooker and tipped the pan this way and that.

The warm oil ran all over the pan.

Suddenly Benjy called out, "Stop! Look! Horses!"

"Horses? Where are the horses?" said Mum.

"On the pan," said Benjy. "Lots of horses with ears and legs."

They both looked at the pan and Mum saw the horses all standing in a crowd together.

Now Benjy had a great idea.
He took a thick sheet of white paper and
he put a big blob of brown paint on it.
Next he put a blob of wet blue paint,
then one of black paint.
Then he tipped the sheet of paper just as
his Mum had tipped the pan.
And there was the picture of a crowd of
horses, brown horses, blue horses,
black horses, all standing together in
a crowd with long legs and listening ears.

Benjy took his painting to school.
"Very good! Very, very good!"
said Miss Wills. "Look children.
Benjy has painted a crowd of horses."
She pinned the painting on the wall.
It was the first time Benjy had ever had
a picture hung up in the classroom.

Now Benjy paints a lot of pictures.
When he puts a brush full of yellow paint
on the paper, he sees sunflowers, so
he gives them black middles.
When he uses blue-green paint,
it looks like the sea.
Then he puts other little bits in his pictures
like the masts of ships sailing on the sea,
or the eye for a pirate,
or a crocodile's sharp teeth,
or leaves for flowers.

Benjy's pictures are not like the pictures of
other children. Why should they be?
When Benjy starts to paint, he puts
a lot of wet paint on the paper.
He tips the paper this way and that and
when the paint runs, Benjy looks to see
what shapes the paint makes before
he thinks what to call his picture.
Why don't you try to see if **you** can make
one of Benjy's pictures?